SUPERTATO

For my lovely Dad

Thank you to Wanda Linnet for her robot picture

SIMON AND SCHUSTER
First published in Great Britain in 2014
by Simon and Schuster UK Ltd
1st Floor, 222 Gray's Inn Road, London, WC1X 8HB
A CBS Company

Text and illustrations copyright © 2014 Sue Hendra
By Paul Linnet and Sue Hendra

A CIP catalogue record for this book is available
from the British Library upon request

978-1-4711-2265-1 (HB)
978-0-85707-447-8 (PB)
978-1-4711-2225-5 (eBook)

Printed in China
1 3 5 7 9 10 8 6 4 2

SUPERTATO

by Sue Hendra

SIMON AND SCHUSTER

London   New York   Sydney   Toronto   New Delhi

Some vegetables are frozen for a very good reason. Don't believe me? Then keep reading.

It was night-time in the supermarket and all was quiet. But –

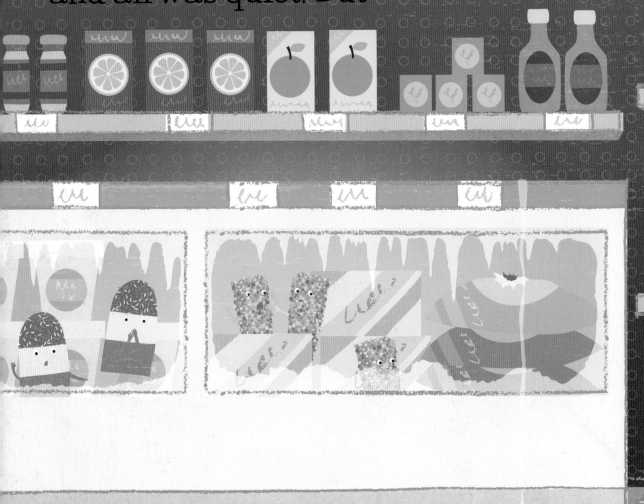

crash, bang – something had escaped from the freezer.
Something small and round and green.

Something looking for trouble.
Big trouble.

"Hmmmmpfff!" cried Cucumber.

Who was doing this? And was there anyone who could help these vegetables in distress?

He used his
super speed . . .

He used his
super strength . . .

He used a flannel
and some soapy water.

"I know who's behind this," said Supertato.
"There's a pea on the loose!"
"Oh no – not a pea!" everyone gasped.

"Yes, a pea! But I'm out of the freezer now and I'm never going back! Mwah ha ha ha ha!" And the evil pea ran off to commit more terrible crimes.

"Time for a dip, little veggies!"

"That's enough!"
shouted Supertato.

He leapt towards
the pea, but the pea
popped out of his
hands and vanished
into thin air.

Supertato set out on a super search.
He crept through the cakes . . .

checked the cheese . . .

and snuck up on the beans.
Then something
caught his eye.

"The game's up!" yelled Supertato.

KERPOW!

But the pea bounced out of reach and onto a trolley. Supertato was just about to stop him with his super strength

 when the trolley crashed –

and he was thrown down into
the icy depths of the freezer.

Was this the end for Supertato?

GASP!

Not quite.

But the pea was off his trolley and lying in wait. "You're finished, Supertato!" he shrieked.

But Supertato summoned up all his strength . . .

and ran for it.

The pea nearly had him at the beans,

and closed in on him at the cheese.

He had him cornered at the cakes.

"So much for Supertato!" screeched the pea.
"You're about to be MASHED POTATO!"

Surely THIS was the end for Supertato?

"Not today, my friend," said Supertato.

"Gotcha!"

"Mmmppfff!" said the pea.

S Q U

"Oh yes," said Supertato.
"I set my trap and you
fell for it. Or should
that be IN it?!" And he
grinned a super grin.

Supertato had saved the day.
"Take him away," he said.
And the pea was marched back
to the freezer where he belonged.

"This jelly tastes of pea!" said Broccoli. And everybody laughed and cheered.

So, remember, folks . . .

Some vegetables are frozen for
a very good reason. Maybe you'd
better go and check your freezer. Just
in case there's an escapee in your house . . .